A Note to Parents

For many children, learning math is difficult and "I hate math!" is their first response — to which many parents silently add "Me, too!" Children often see adults comfortably reading and writing, but they rarely have such models for mathematics. And math fear can be catching!

The easy-to-read stories in this **Hello Math Reader!** series were written to give children a positive introduction to mathematics, and parents a pleasurable re-acquaintance with a subject that is important to everyone's life. **Hello Math Reader!** stories make mathematical ideas accessible, interesting, and fun for children. The activities and suggestions at the end of each book provide parents with a hands-on approach to help children develop mathematical interest and confidence.

Enjoy the mathematics!
• Give your child a chance to retell the story. The more familiar children are with the story, the more they will understand its mathematical concepts.
• Use the colorful illustrations to help children "hear and see" the math at work in the story.
• Treat the math activities as games to be played for fun. Follow your child's lead. Spend time on those activities that engage your child's interest and curiosity.
• Activities, especially ones using physical materials, help make abstract mathematical ideas concrete.

Learning is a messy process. Learning about math calls for children to become immersed in lively experiences that help them make sense of mathematical concepts and symbols.

Although learning about numbers is basic to math, other ideas, such as identifying shapes and patterns, measuring, collecting and interpreting data, reasoning logically, and thinking about chance, are also important. By reading these stories and having fun with the activities, you will help your child enthusiastically say "**Hello, math**," instead of "I hate math."

—Marilyn Burns
National Mathematics Educator
Author of *The I Hate Mathematics! Book*

To my sister Kim
— A.B.

To Mark and Daniel,
for many pots of hearty soup shared.
Thank you.
— K.A.J.

ISBN 0-439-16966-6

Library of Congress Cataloging-in-Publication Data

Buckless, Andrea.
    Too many cooks!/ by Andrea Buckless; illustrated by Kayne Jacobs ; math activities by Marilyn Burns
        p.   cm. — (Hello Math reader! Level 3)
    Summary: Cara and her two younger brothers have fun using multiplication to make a very unusual soup for the family dinner.
    ISBN 0-439-16966-6
    [1. Multiplication — Fiction. 2. Cookery — Fiction. 3. Brothers and sisters — Fiction. 4. Humorous stories.] I. Jacobs, Kayne, ill. II. Burns, Marilyn, III. Title. IV. Series.

PZ7.B8817 To 2001
[E]—dc21   99-087694
                                                                                                          CIP

10 9 8 7 6 5 4   03   04

Printed in the U.S.A.   23
First printing, November 2000

Too Many Cooks!

by Andrea Buckless • Illustrated by K.A. Jacobs
Math Activities by Marilyn Burns

Hello Math Reader! — Level 3

SCHOLASTIC INC.
New York   Toronto   London   Auckland   Sydney
Mexico City   New Delhi   Hong Kong

Cara was baby-sitting her two brothers,
Jay and Marcos.
Jay held his book up to Cara.
"Read it to me *again*, pleasssse!" he said.

"When is Mom coming home?"
Marcos asked.
"Soon," Cara said. "She went
to get Grandma and Grandpa."
"Read! Read! Read!" Jay wailed.
"I'm bored," Marcos sighed.
"I have an idea," said Cara.

Cara pulled out a cookbook.
"Let's surprise everybody," she said.
"Let's make dinner!" She flipped
through the book.
"There are three of us, plus Mom,
plus Grandma and Grandpa," Cara said.
"3 + 1 + 2. That makes six people."

"Let's make soup!" said Marcos.
"Super-duper soup!" yelled Jay.
He threw his hands in the air.
The book went flying, right into his milk.
The glass tipped over.
The soup recipe got soaked.

"I think I can still read the recipe,"
Cara said.
Marcos looked at the soggy page.
"Are you sure?" he asked.
Cara looked at the book again. It *was*
hard to read.
"I think it says to start with two tomatoes,"
she said.
Marcos dropped two tomatoes into
the pot.

The pot did not look very full.
"Let's try two tomatoes for each person,"
he said.
"6 x 2 is 12." He put in ten more tomatoes.
"That looks better," Cara said.
Marcos and Cara gave each other
high fives.
Jay tossed a red rubber ball into the pot.

"Next, onions," Cara read. "Should we double again?"
Marcos held his nose. "No. Onions smell bad. Let's just put in one for each of us."
"Okay," said Cara. "3 x 1 is 3 onions for us."
"I meant *all* of us," said Marcos.

He counted out three more onions. Marcos and Cara did a little dance. Jay danced, too. Then he dropped a few blocks into the pot.

Cara looked at the cookbook.
"This part is really wet," she said.
"All I can see is the word *carrots*."

Marcos got out a bag of baby carrots.
"10, 20, 30, 40, 50," he counted.
"That should do it," Marcos said.

"Don't forget yourself," Cara said.
Marcos threw another ten baby carrots
into the soup.
He and Cara made bunny ears at each other.
Jay hopped up and down.
He put two orange cars into the pot.

Cara read the recipe again.
"We need two beets for each person,"
she said.
"Yuck!" said Marcos. "I don't like beets!"
"6 x 0 is 0," said Cara. "NO beets in
the soup!"
"0 + 0 + 0 + 0 + 0 + 0 is still 0!"
shouted Marcos.
"NO beets in the soup!"
Jay banged the pot lids.
"No beets, no beets!" he yelled.

"I can read this next part," Cara said.
"We need two cups of beans."
She handed Marcos the beans and a cup.
Then she went to find a big spoon.

Marcos poured two cups of beans into
the soup.
"Did Cara mean two cups for each person?"
he said.
"6 of us times 2 cups each makes 12 cups."
Marcos kept pouring.
A dozen cups of beans sank
to the bottom of the pot.

Marcos went to find Cara.
Jay filled the cup with blue marbles.
They sank to the bottom of the soup pot —
so did his green dinosaur
and his yellow bulldozer.

Cara bent over the cookbook.
"Add wide noodles," she read.
"How much?" asked Marcos.
"The book says to follow the directions
on the noodle bag," said Cara.
"Mom keeps the noodles in a glass jar,"
said Marcos.
Cara thought for a minute.
"How about five noodles for each person?"
she asked.

Marcos grabbed a handful of noodles.
"5, 10, 15, 20, 25, 30," he counted.
"Or 5 + 5 + 5 + 5 + 5 + 5," Cara chanted.
"Or 6 x 5 is 30!" they both sang.
Jay sang, too.
Then he put some yellow string into the pot.

Cara checked the cookbook once more.
Marcos looked for the pot lid.
Jay climbed into the cupboard.

"Noodles, noodles," he whispered.
He got out a bag of gummy worms.
When no one was looking, he dropped
the wiggly candy worms into the pot.

"Now we need to cook the soup,"
Cara said.
"Everybody step back, please."
She put the pot of soup on the stove.
The pot was very full.
Soup splashed over the top.
It ran down the sides of the pot.
Cara clamped the lid on.
"There," she said. "Now, let's set the table."

Cara counted out six soup bowls.
Marcos grabbed six soup spoons.
Jay bunched up the napkins.
Then he put a wrinkled one at each place.
"Something smells funny," said Marcos.

"Hello! We're here!" someone called.
"What smells so funny?" someone
else asked.

Mom, Grandma, and Grandpa walked in.
"Surprise!" the three children shouted.
"We made dinner," Marcos said.
"Please sit down, and I will bring you
each a bowl," Cara said.

Everyone sat down.
Cara quickly filled the bowls.
"Hmmm. I love soup," Grandpa said.
He looked into his bowl.
A green dinosaur looked back at him.
"Smells a bit funny," said Grandma,
"but I'll bet it tastes good."
She dipped her spoon into the soup.
Marbles rolled around in her bowl.
Mom pulled out a long, drippy
gummy worm.
"Where did you ever find this recipe?"
she asked.
"Jay!" Cara shouted.
"Jay!" Marcos shouted.

Jay laughed.

A yellow bulldozer floated in his bowl.

"Super-duper soup!" he said.

Grandma and Grandpa smiled.

Mom grinned.

Marcos giggled and Cara chuckled.

"Super-duper soup is right!" she said.

"But could we order pizza for
dinner tonight?"

• ABOUT THE ACTIVITIES •

It's important that children learn to apply math skills to real-world problems. Problems from real life provide contexts for numbers, helping children see how numbers are used in various situations. Also, problems motivate children to reason numerically, giving them a chance to make use of the math skills they are acquiring.

Too Many Cooks! takes place in the kitchen, a familiar setting for children. The story describes how Cara and her two brothers try to make soup for their mother and grandparents. Their effort is sincere and their mathematical reasoning is sound, but their cooking skills are humorously lacking.

Children will enjoy this story, which incorporates both addition and multiplication. They'll also get the chance to think about numerical relationships. Your child may not have been formally introduced to multiplication, but seeing expressions such as "6 x 0" or "6 x 5" in the context of the story will help him or her become familiar with new math symbols and see how multiplication and addition are related to one another.

The activities that follow will give your child more experience with the math concepts at work in the story. Follow your child's interests and have fun with math!

—Marilyn Burns

> You'll find tips and suggestions
> for guiding the activities whenever
> you see a box like this!

Retelling the Story

3 + 1 + 2

Cara figured out that she and her two brothers, Jay and Marcos, needed to make dinner for six people. Cara said, "3 + 1 + 2. That makes six people." What was Cara thinking of when she figured this way?

When Marcos put two tomatoes in the pot, the pot did not look very full, so he wanted to put in two tomatoes for each person: 6 x 2. Marcos figured out that he needed to add ten more tomatoes for all six people. Can you explain why this is right?

Next, Cara and Marcos decided to put in one onion for each person. You could say that 6 x 1 = 6. Do you know what this means?

Carrots came next. Marcos counted ten baby carrots for each person. How many carrots did Marcos put into the pot altogether?

The recipe said to put in two beets for each person. But Cara and Marcos put in zero beets for each person. Why did they do this?

Cara read that they needed two cups of beans for each person. Marcos said, "6 of us times 2 cups each would be 12 cups." Is this right?

Next came noodles. Marcos added five noodles for each person. "6 x 5," Marcos and Cara sang. How many noodles did Marcos put into the pot for six people?

Why do you think the soup smelled funny while it was cooking?

What did the family eat for dinner?

The Magic of Zero

Cara and Marcos decided to use zero beets for each person. For two people, that's zero beets. For three people, that's still zero beets. And for six people, $0 + 0 + 0 + 0 + 0 + 0$ is still 0!

Zero is the easiest number to add because whatever number you add it to doesn't change at all. Here are some examples:

$4 + 0 = 4$
$23 + 0 = 23$
$0 + 100 = 100$
$253 + 0 + 0 + 0 = 253$

Make up some other problems like these.

Making 6

To figure out how many people would be at dinner, Cara added the children (3), her Mom (1), plus Grandma and Grandpa (2). She found that $3 + 1 + 2$ makes 6 people.

If Cara added the number of children (Cara, Marcos, and Jay) and the number of grown-ups (Mom, Grandma, and Grandpa), she would think $3 + 3$.

If Cara added just herself to all the others, she would think $1 + 5$. Each of these ways makes 6:

$3 + 1 + 2 = 6$
$3 + 3 = 6$
$1 + 5 = 6$

What other ways can you think of to add numbers and get 6? Write them down.

Skip Counting

First, Marcos put in two tomatoes for each person. He put in 12 tomatoes altogether: 2, 4, 6, 8, 10, 12. Can you count by 2s? Take 12 beans or pennies, put them into groups of 2, and then try counting them by 2s.

When Marcos was putting baby carrots into the soup, he counted by tens: 10, 20, 30, 40, 50, 60. Can you count by 10s? Take 60 beans or pennies, put them into groups of 10, and then try counting them by 10s.

When Marcos was putting noodles into the soup, he counted by fives: 5, 10, 15, 20, 25, 30. Can you count by 5s? Take 30 beans or pennies, put them into groups of 5, and then try counting them by 5s.

If your child hasn't learned to count by 2s, 5s, and 10s, then count out loud slowly and invite him or her to count along with you. Using beans or pennies helps your child see that each number represents a group of objects.

Soup That Tastes Good

Maybe you'd like to cook up some soup for your family. (Make sure you do this *only* with a parent, adult, or older sibling.) If you like chicken noodle soup, here's how to make enough for about four people. You will need to measure out:

2 cups chicken broth or bouillon
1/2 cup carrots, chopped into small pieces
1 stalk of celery, chopped into small pieces
1 tablespoon butter or margarine
1/2 teaspoon salt
1/4 teaspoon poultry seasoning
1/2 cup thin egg noodles

Melt the butter or margarine in a saucepan. Add the carrots and celery, and cook over low heat until they are soft. Add the chicken broth, salt, and poultry seasoning, and bring to a boil. Add the noodles, and cook until they are soft.

Yum, yum!